EMPIRE
BUILDERS

Julie Haydon

THOMSON

NELSON

Australia · Canada · Mexico · Singapore · Spain · United Kingdom · United States

RULING AN EMPIRE

Countries like Australia, New Zealand, the United States of America, England, India and Japan are **democracies**. The word democracy means 'rule by the people'. In a democracy, the government is voted into office by the people.

These children live in a democracy. When they grow up, they will be able to vote for their choice of government.

In the past, many of the countries we know today were grouped together to form **empires**. An empire was often ruled by a single person called an emperor or empress. The ruler was very powerful, and decided how people would live and what laws they had to obey.

Some emperors and empresses changed the world by expanding their empires and achieving great things.

Three people who successfully ruled empires were:

**Catherine the Great
(1729 to 1796)**

**Alexander the Great
(356 to 323 BC)**

**Charlemagne
(742 to 814)**

ALEXANDER THE

Alexander the Great was born in 356 BC. His parents were the King and Queen of Macedonia.

Alexander spent most of his childhood at the royal palace in Pella, the capital. He was an intelligent, energetic child. He was taught science, medicine, **literature** and other subjects. He also trained as a soldier and ruler.

A sculpture of
Alexander the Great.

GREAT

Even as a child, Alexander longed for glory. His father was a fine soldier and ruler, who won many battles and expanded his territory to include many Greek cities. Alexander worried that his father would leave him nothing to **conquer**.

Alexander was a keen student.

When Alexander was a boy, his father was offered an expensive horse, Bucephalas. The horse was uncontrollable and no one could mount it. Alexander made a bet with his father that he could ride the horse. Alexander calmed the horse, then mounted and rode it before his proud father. Alexander kept the horse for twenty years and rode him into many battles. When Bucephalas died, Alexander named a city after him.

In 336 BC, the king was killed. Twenty-year-old Alexander inherited the kingdom. Alexander quickly dealt with enemies in Macedonia and in areas his father had conquered. Then he turned his attention to conquering the **Persian Empire**.

In 334 BC, Alexander began his war against Persia. Alexander was a military genius. He won the first battle.

Alexander and his army.

Alexander in Egypt.

The following year, Alexander's army fought the King of Persia's army and won. The King of Persia, Darius, fled, leaving his family behind. Alexander took Darius's family captive, but he treated them with respect and kindness.

Alexander travelled to Egypt, where the people greeted him warmly. He founded the city of Alexandria at the mouth of the Nile River.

Alexander defeated Darius and his army again in 331 BC. Darius escaped and was later killed by his own men.

Moving on to Persepolis, an important city in Persia, Alexander took the riches from the palace **treasury**, then burned the palace to the ground.

Alexander continued his conquest of the Persian Empire. It took him eight years.

He entered India and would have continued his exploration except his men refused to go any further. They wanted to go home. Reluctantly, Alexander turned back.

The ruins of Persepolis.

Alexander and his army head home.

The sarcuphagus, or stone coffin, of Alexander.

Alexander was more than just a ruthless conqueror. He built new cities. He respected the customs and traditions of the people he conquered. And he encouraged his soldiers to marry Persian women. Alexander married three times. He had two sons, but both died young.

Alexander died on the journey home in 323 BC. He was 32 when he died. It is believed he died of a fever.

Alexander's achievements include:

- conquering the Persian Empire

- building new cities

- spreading the Greek language and culture

- encouraging the merging of cultures

- establishing standard coins to be used throughout his empire

- improving trade throughout his empire

- encouraging the studying of **geography** and science

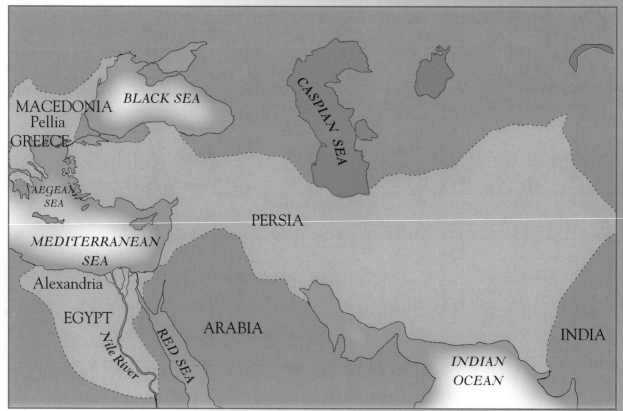

The orange areas of this map show Alexander's empire at its greatest.

CHARLEMAGNE

In 768, the King of the Franks died. His empire, which covered most of present-day France, Belgium, the Netherlands, Switzerland and Germany, was divided between his sons, Carloman and Charlemagne.

When Carloman died suddenly in 771, 29-year-old Charlemagne became the sole ruler.

Charlemagne's real name was Charles. Charlemagne means Charles the Great.

A sculpture of Charlemagne.

11

Charlemagne made plans to expand his kingdom. He used his powerful army to invade a region called Saxony. The Saxons had been raiding the Frankish borders. The Franks and the Saxons fought against each other many times. The Saxons were **pagans**, not **Christians** like the Franks. Charlemagne wanted to **convert** the Saxons to Christianity. It took more than 30 years before Charlemagne was successful.

In the early years of his reign, Charlemagne often treated the Saxons harshly. Once he had 4500 Saxon prisoners **executed** in one day.

Charlemagne's sword was called Joyeuse.

Frankish horsemen.

tame · Et puis comment
taxilles li dus de baiuiere
li fit homage · Et comet
ces gens furent descomfit
en saxoigne ꝝ   vi

lan · Thommas li archeues
ques de la ville baptisa et
leua de fons une seue fille·
ces peres fu esperitueux et
li mist anon Gille · Arrant

A document that shows Charlemagne meeting the Pope.

Charlemagne was an active man. He liked horse riding, hunting and swimming. He was a skilled warrior, but he was also a religious man. In 773, the **pope**'s lands in central Italy were attacked by the Lombards from northern Italy. Charlemagne's army fought the Lombards and won. The Lombard king was sent to a monastery for the rest of his life. Charlemagne became King of the Lombards.

The Franks fought many other wars and won more land. In 800, the pope gave Charlemagne the title of Emperor of the Romans. When the pope gave Charlemagne this title, people knew the pope approved of Charlemagne ruling part of Italy and other areas in Western Europe.

Yet Charlemagne was more than just a warrior-king. He valued education and progress and he wanted peace for his people and lands.

Frankish kings before Charlemagne had moved from place to place, taking their **court** with them. Charlemagne established a capital at Aachen and built a palace and a church there.

Charlemagne invited scholars and artists to his palace. He had libraries and schools set up. Hand-written copies were made of important books, accounts and records.

Charlemagne also made changes to the laws. He ordered that the laws of many of the peoples he had conquered be written down. He included some of these laws in the laws of his empire.

Charlemagne, Emperor of the Romans.

Even as an adult, Charlemagne liked learning. He studied mathematics, **grammar**, **astronomy**, music and other subjects.

A document signed by Charlemagne.

Charlemagne's empire was so large that he appointed other people to look after districts. Charlemagne met with these people once or twice a year to discuss problems and plans.

Charlemagne was married four times and had many children.

Charlemagne loved his children and liked to spend time with them. He died in 814.

Charlemagne and one of his wives.

Charlemagne's son Louis ruled the empire after Charlemagne's death.

Charlemagne's achievements include:

- uniting most of Western Europe in one empire
- establishing good relations with other powerful rulers outside his empire
- improving the laws
- encouraging trade
- establishing libraries and preserving many old texts
- building roads and bridges
- setting up schools
- giving money to the poor
- inventing a system of weights, measures and coins to be used throughout his empire

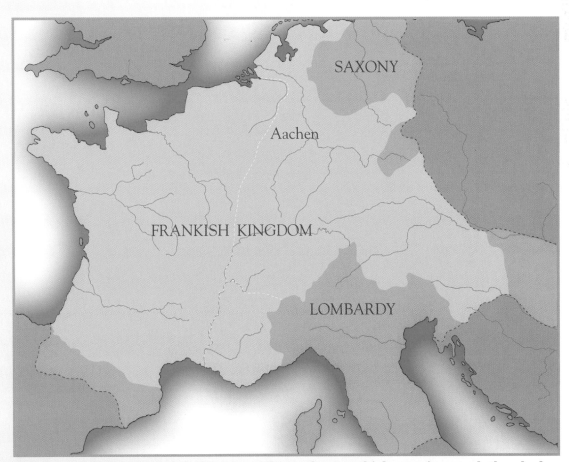

The pale orange areas of this map show the Frankish empire, and the dark orange areas were added under Charlemagne's rule.

CATHERINE THE

In 1744, a 15-year-old German princess became engaged to the **heir** to the Russian throne, Peter. The princess's name was Sophia, but her name was changed to Catherine the day before the engagement was announced.

A painting of Catherine the Great.

Catherine was intelligent and confident. She wanted to be Empress of Russia one day, so she worked hard to fit into her new country and her new role. She learnt Russian. She changed her religion. She did her best to please the empress, Peter's aunt.

Catherine travelled to Russia with her mother and several servants in horse-drawn coaches. Once inside Russia, the empress sent them sleighs full of furs and silk mattresses. Each sleigh was pulled by ten horses.

GREAT

Catherine and Peter were married in 1745, but their marriage was not a happy one. Peter was sickly, weak and childish. Catherine had no real work to do, and she was bored. She spent a lot of time riding horses, hunting and dancing. She also read widely. Many of the books she read made her think about the best way a country should be ruled.

Catherine gave birth to a son, Paul, in 1754.

A painting of Emperor Peter III.

Catherine enjoyed horse-riding.

When Peter became the emperor in 1762, he was unpopular. Peter was born in Germany. He never felt Russian and had little interest in the country. He did not know how to rule well. He made bad decisions that upset many people. Peter also wanted to get rid of Catherine. Catherine knew she was in danger, so she took action. Several months after Peter became the emperor, Catherine took over. Peter was taken prisoner. He died later that year.

Catherine became Empress in 1762.

Catherine's palace in St Petersburg.

Over the next 34 years, Catherine would rule Russia as Empress Catherine II. Catherine worked hard to expand Russia's territory through wars and agreements with other countries. She also made Russia a more modern country.

Catherine encouraged education and **culture**. She was very keen on literature and journalism and encouraged the development of the Russian **publishing** industry. Catherine did not succeed in making huge changes to Russian laws, but she did encourage discussions about law **reform**.

But not everyone benefited under Catherine's rule. The Russian peasants, called **serfs**, lived miserable lives. Serfs were forced to work for Russian nobles. Catherine was aware of how badly the serfs were treated and did not like it, but she did little to help them. The support of the nobles was too important to her.

Catherine did not remarry after Peter died. She died in 1796.

Catherine's son Paul ruled the empire after her death.

Serfs were forced to work for Russian Nobles.

Catherine's achievements include:

- winning two major wars and expanding Russia's territory

- improving trade routes

- building new towns and ports

- building schools and promoting education

- building hospitals and promoting healthcare

- encouraging immigration to fill areas of unpopulated land

- encouraging the use of new farming techniques

- encouraging the creation and publication of Russian literature

- improving Russia's image amongst other nations

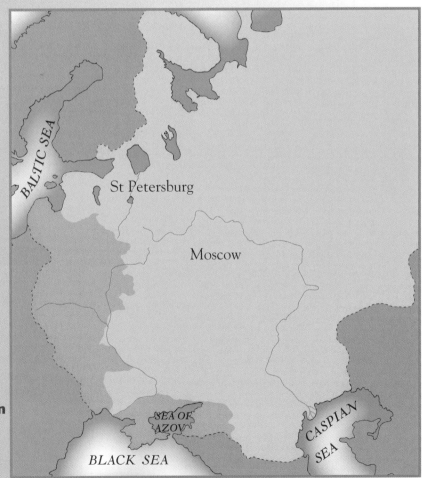

The pale orange areas of this map show the Russian empire, and the dark orange areas were added under Catherine's rule.

GLOSSARY

astronomy	the study of the planets, stars, moon and sun
Christians	people who believe in the religion of Jesus Christ
conquer	to overcome by force
convert	to change religious beliefs from one faith to another
court	the people who work and live with a monarch
culture	the arts, such as music, literature, painting and dance
democracies	countries where the people vote for the government
empires	countries grouped together under the rule of an emperor or empress
executed	killed under order
geography	the study of the earth's surface and its features (such as rivers, mountains and deserts), climate, plants and populations
grammar	the way the words of a language are combined to make sentences, headings etc.
heir	the person in line to inherit the throne
literature	high-quality writing, such as books and plays
pagans	people who did not follow the Christian faith
Persian Empire	the most powerful empire in the world before Alexander the Great conquered it
pope	the head of the Catholic church
publishing	the printing and binding of books and plays etc.
reform	changes for the better
serfs	Russian peasants who were forced to work for nobles
treasury	a building where the coins, gold, and other treasures of a city or country were kept
unpopular	not popular

INDEX